NODDY

The Case of
the Hiding Pirates

Hodder
Children's
Books

There's a **pirate parade** happening in Toyland today! The pirates are going to play their instruments and sing a new song.

"Aye-aye, me hearties!" says Pat-Pat. "I can't wait for the ..."

"Pirate parade!" cheer the Pockets.

"Oh dear," Big Ears sighs. "It's so noisy already."

Poor Big Ears. Pirate parades are **meant** to be noisy! We've got streamers and flags and balloons. We're just missing one thing ...

... pirates!

Where are the pirates?

WOOF! WOOF!

Bumpy points his nose towards the sky. A bird flies down and lands on my finger. It's Scurvy, the parrot!

"Hello," I say. "Where are the pirate crew?"

"Hiding! Hiding!" squawks Scurvy.

The toys gasp. Why are the pirates hiding? What about the parade? I need to investigate! I'm going to call this the Case of the Hiding Pirates.

Deltoid leaps into the air. He is ready for action!

"Hey, Noddy!" he shouts. "The pirates are my neighbours in DareDale. I am determined to help."

"Thanks," I reply. "Let's start by talking to Scurvy."

Deltoid runs over to Scurvy.

"Did the pirates tell you why they are hiding?" he asks.

"Please be quiet!" squawks Scurvy. "Please be quiet!"

What a strange reply!

I know! If we can find out **where** the pirates are hiding, perhaps we can find out why they are hiding.

Bumpy and I jump into Revs. Deltoid climbs in the back.

"Scurvy!" I call. "Come with us!"

Revs drives us to the pirates' galleon. Scurvy squawks and shouts all the way. "Squawk. Squawk. **Squawk!**"

What a noisy car ride!

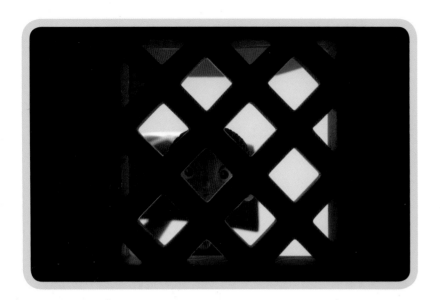

I open a trapdoor in the galleon. It is where the pirates keep their musical instruments.

"Oh!" I gasp. "The instrument cases are empty!"

"First Mate Stripes?" squawks Scurvy. **"Pirate Captain?"**

"Don't worry," says Deltoid. "We'll find the pirates, then we can have the parade."

Bumpy sniffs around underneath the galleon. Woof! **Woof!**

Clever Bumpy. He has found a map of the DareDale Caves. The caves are the perfect pirate hiding place.

"Let's go!" I shout.

The ride to the DareDale Caves gets even noisier. Scurvy won't stop squawking!

"Do you think you could sing a little bit more quietly?" I ask.

It is dark inside the caves. Deltoid lifts up a crystal. There's something small and thin underneath it.

"BANG! BANG! BANG!" shouts Scurvy.

"That's right, Scurvy," I laugh. "It's a drumstick."

The pirates must be playing their instruments. Maybe we can hear them? Deltoid and I try to listen.

"Please be quiet!" squawks Scurvy.

"We are the pirates of the sea, and a merry band are we …"

That sounds like pirate music! I listen again. **"Please be quiet!"** screeches Scurvy.

"Please stop squawking," begs Deltoid.

It is so noisy with Scurvy around!

I wonder if the pirates had this trouble with Scurvy too? That must be why they are hiding!

Deltoid takes Scurvy back to Toy Green. The next part of this investigation needs some quiet.

How am I going to find the pirates? Simple. By being quiet and listening out for their music!

Bumpy and I wait for the tune to start again.

"We are the pirates of the sea, and a merry band are we ..."

"The pirates!" I cry. "This way!"

We run through the caves, following the sound. We dash around a corner and ...

"Ahoy, Noddy," says Pirate Captain. "We didn't think you'd find us here."

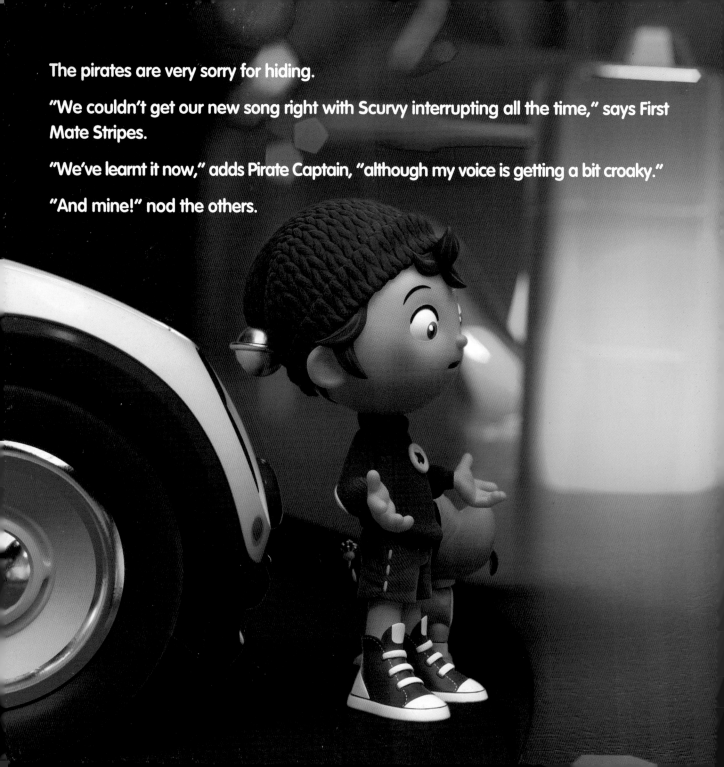

The pirates are very sorry for hiding.

"We couldn't get our new song right with Scurvy interrupting all the time," says First Mate Stripes.

"We've learnt it now," adds Pirate Captain, "although my voice is getting a bit croaky."

"And mine!" nod the others.

This sounds like a job for ...

Noddy, Toyland Detective!

I've got an idea that will help the pirates' voices and let Scurvy join in. It's time to go back to Toy Green.

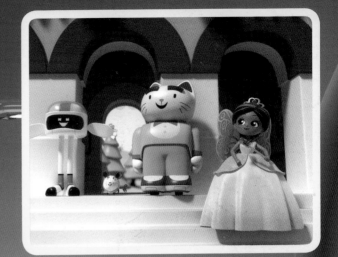

Everybody in Toyland comes to join the pirate parade. There are balloons, flags and streamers! The galleon leads the way.

"We are the pirates of the sea," sing the pirates.

"We are the pirates of the sea," squawks Scurvy.

"And a merry band are we!"

"And a merry band are we!" squawks Scurvy.

Everybody cheers. What a merry tune!

Scurvy sings the song over and over again.

Everyone enjoys the noisy parade, even Big Ears.

"Well done, Noddy," he says. "You found the pirates."

A picture pops up on my **Who-What-Where Book**.

"I thought Scurvy was shouting, but he was trying to help me all along," I explain. "The pirates were only hiding so they could practise their song."

"Ooh-argh, me hearties!" pipes up the pirate parrot.

Good old Scurvy! The Case of the Hiding Pirates is **closed!**

Hodder Children's Books

First published in Great Britain in 2017 by Hodder and Stoughton
Noddy © 2017 DreamWorks Distribution Limited. All Rights Reserved.

The moral rights of the author and illustrator have been asserted.

A CIP catalogue record of this book is available from
the British Library.

ISBN 978 1 444 93297 3

10 9 8 7 6 5 4 3 2 1

Printed and bound in Europe

MIX
Paper from
responsible sources
FSC® C104740

Hodder Children's Books
An imprint of Hachette Children's Group
Part of Hodder and Stoughton
Carmelite House
50 Victoria Embankment
London EC4Y 0DZ

An Hachette UK Company
www.hachettechildrens.co.uk
www.hachette.co.uk